W9-CHJ-688

W9-CHJ-688

Take me out to the Ball game

Maryann Kovalski

SCHOLASTIC
HARDCOVER

SCHOLASTIC INC./NEW YORK

Jenny and Joanna were baseball mad.
"Play ball!" they would call to anyone they could find.

Fly balls, grounders. Pitch, hit, slide. "You're out!"
Then, "One more game!" they'd shout.

Only one call could make a game stall
and Grandma's came one day —

"I'd like to know where you want to go?"
And snap! like that they sang . . .

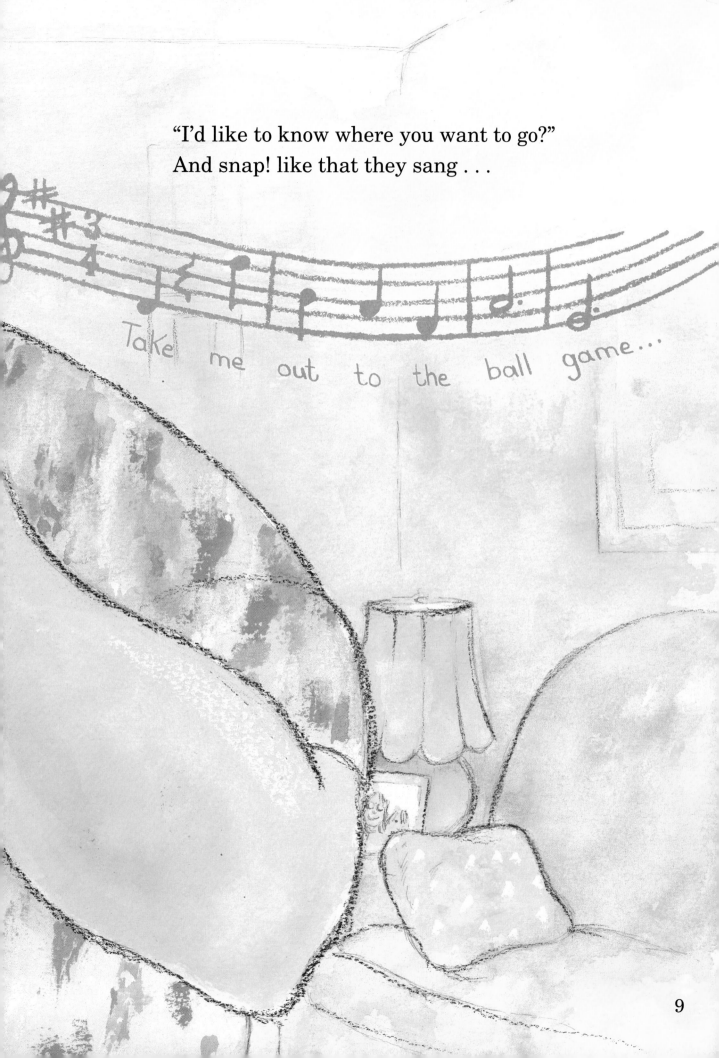

Take me out to the ball game...

Take me out to the ball game,

10

take me out to the crowd!

Buy me some peanuts and Cracker Jack,

I don't care if I never get back!

Let me root, root, root for the home team,

19

if they don't win it's a shame!

For it's one . . .

two . . .

three strikes —

"You're out!"

At the old ball game!

Take Me Out to the Ball Game

Words by Jack Norworth

Music by Albert von Tilzer

Take me out to the ball game,

Take me out to the crowd._____

Buy me some pea - nuts and crack - er jack

I don't care if I nev- er come back, Let me

root, root, root for the home team, If

they don't win it's a shame._____ For it's

one, two, three strikes, "You're out!" at the

old ball game. _____

For Gail

Originally published in 1992 in Canada
by Scholastic Canada Limited.

Copyright © 1992 by Maryann Kovalski.

All rights reserved. Published by Scholastic Inc.,
730 Broadway, New York, NY 10003, by arrangement with
North Winds Press, an imprint of Scholastic Canada Limited.

SCHOLASTIC HARDCOVER is a registered trademark of Scholastic Inc.

No part of this publication may be reproduced in whole or in part, or
stored in a retrieval system, or transmitted in any form or by any
means, electronic, mechanical, photocopying, recording, or otherwise,
without written permission of the publisher. For information
regarding permission, write to North Winds Press, an imprint of
Scholastic Canada Limited, 123 Newkirk Road, Richmond Hills, Ontario,
Canada L4C 3G5.

Library of Congress Cataloging-in-Publication Data

Kovalski, Maryann.
Take me out to the ballgame / by Maryann Kovalski.
p. cm.
Summary: The lyrics of the familiar song, with illustrations
showing two baseball-mad girls enjoying a ballgame with their
grandmother.
ISBN 0-590-45638-5
1. Children's song—Texts. [1. Baseball—Songs and music.
2. Songs.] I. Title.
PZ8.3K8535Tak 1993
782.42164´0268—dc20   92-10155
                                                 CIP
                                                  AC

12 11 10 9 8 7 6 5 4 3 2 1   3 4 5 6 8/9

Printed in the U.S.A.   36

First Scholastic printing, April 1993